CASPAR

AND THE SECRET KINGDOM

Caspar the cat came prowling
and growling,
Lord of the jungle, stalking his prey.
Where he has come from or
where he is going,
Caspar the cat is not ready to say…

CASPAR
AND THE SECRET KINGDOM

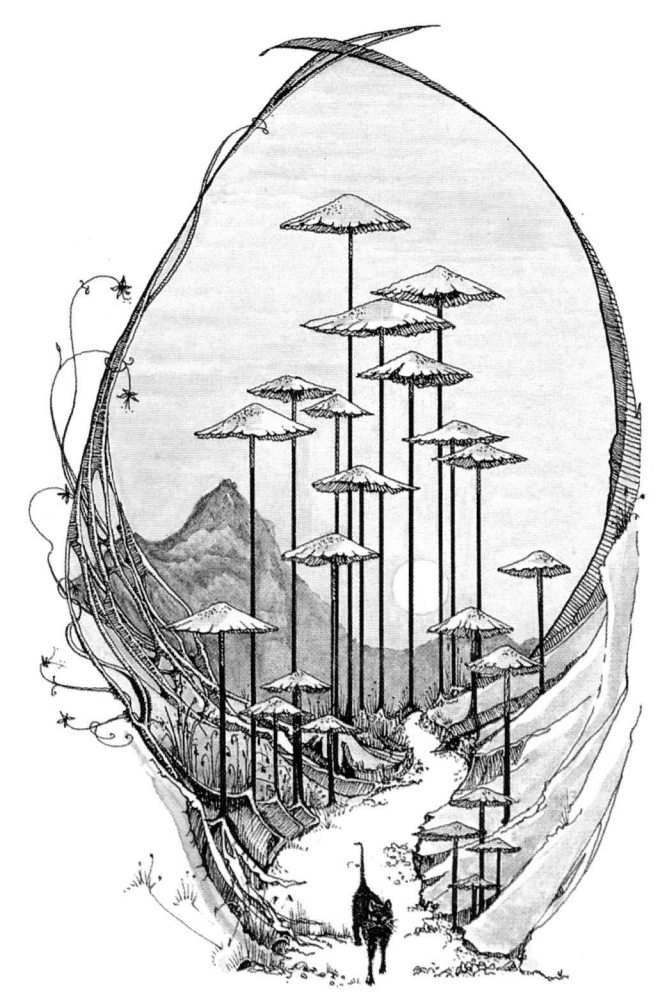

Illustrated by
LOIS ALLARD

Written by
MIRANDA SEYMOUR

SILVER BURDETT COMPANY · MORRISTOWN, NEW JERSEY

Published in the United States
in 1986 by Silver Burdett Company
Morristown, New Jersey

First published in Great Britain 1986 by
Beehive Books, an imprint of
Macdonald & Co. (Publishers) Ltd
Greater London House, Hampstead Road.
London NW1 7QX

A BPCC plc company

Illustrations © Lois Allard 1986
Text © Miranda Seymour 1986

Printed in Spain

Library of Congress Cataloging-in-Publication Data

Seymour, Miranda.
    Caspar and the secret kingdom.

    Summary: Caspar the black cat follows an underground route
to find the Secret Kingdom of the Cats, where his encounter
with a huge dragon promises to release the feline inhabitants
from being frozen in eternal winter.
    [1. Cats–Fiction.   2. Dragons–Fiction.   3. Fantasy]
I. Allard, Lois, Ill.   II. Title.
P27.S524Cas 1987   [E]   86-6674
ISBN 0-382-09307-0

Caspar the cat is small and black – black paws, black ears, black tail and eyes that shine like moons from the depths of a small, black face. He is the sort of cat you might meet any time, anywhere, going about his business in a purposeful way. But where he is going and where he has come from, you can never be perfectly sure. He may have been on an adventure. He may have been sound asleep. For Caspar is a mysterious cat and keeps these things a secret.

Caspar did not think of himself as a small, black cat. Oh no. When he went for a walk, he was lord of the jungle, a tiger stalking its prey. One mighty roar from Caspar the fearless had lions quaking before him. The grass bent down beneath his kingly paws. Small birds fled from his royal path. And Caspar, who was not actually very brave at all, felt every inch a hero as he prowled in the tangly woods.

5

One summer evening, Caspar was padding along a woodland path, wondering where to have a catnap, when he came to a spot that looked just right. It was deep in the heart of the wood, a shady hollow thickly overgrown. He was about to settle down when something made him look more closely at the ground. The roots that spread out from an old tree appeared to be moving. He looked again. The roots were alive! Scaly branches were wriggling through the undergrowth and – stranger still – tiny buildings appeared to be sprouting from the tree itself.

Caspar crouched, one paw tapping the largest root. Then, slowly, slowly he slid forward, creeping like a panther until he was near enough to peep over the top. What was this? Caspar found himself looking at a flight of steps that led deep down into the heart of the tree.

Cats are cautious creatures, but curious, and Caspar was no exception. He put all thoughts of sleep behind him and, feeling just a little frightened but eager to discover what lay at the bottom of the steps, he jumped over the root and started to follow the staircase down.

Round and round, down and down went the spiral stairway, curling so tightly round itself that Caspar could never see further in front than the next bend or further behind than the last.

Round and round, down and down, deep into the darkness he padded, until at last he reached the bottom. He had come into a vast and earthy cave, webbed round by the oldest roots of the tree. In every direction there were tunnels: tunnels like cavernous sockets where invisible eyes gazed, watching his every move; tunnels like gaping mouths waiting for him to walk in.

Caspar's fur prickled with fear. It wasn't easy to think of himself as lord of the jungle in this cold and silent world. He tried a small growl, and jumped when a thousand echoes boomed back at him from every side. Feeling more like a mouse than a fearless king of the beasts, he crept towards one of the tunnels where he could just make out the faintest glimmer of light, and entered its open mouth. Through the creaking darkness, he made his way forward.

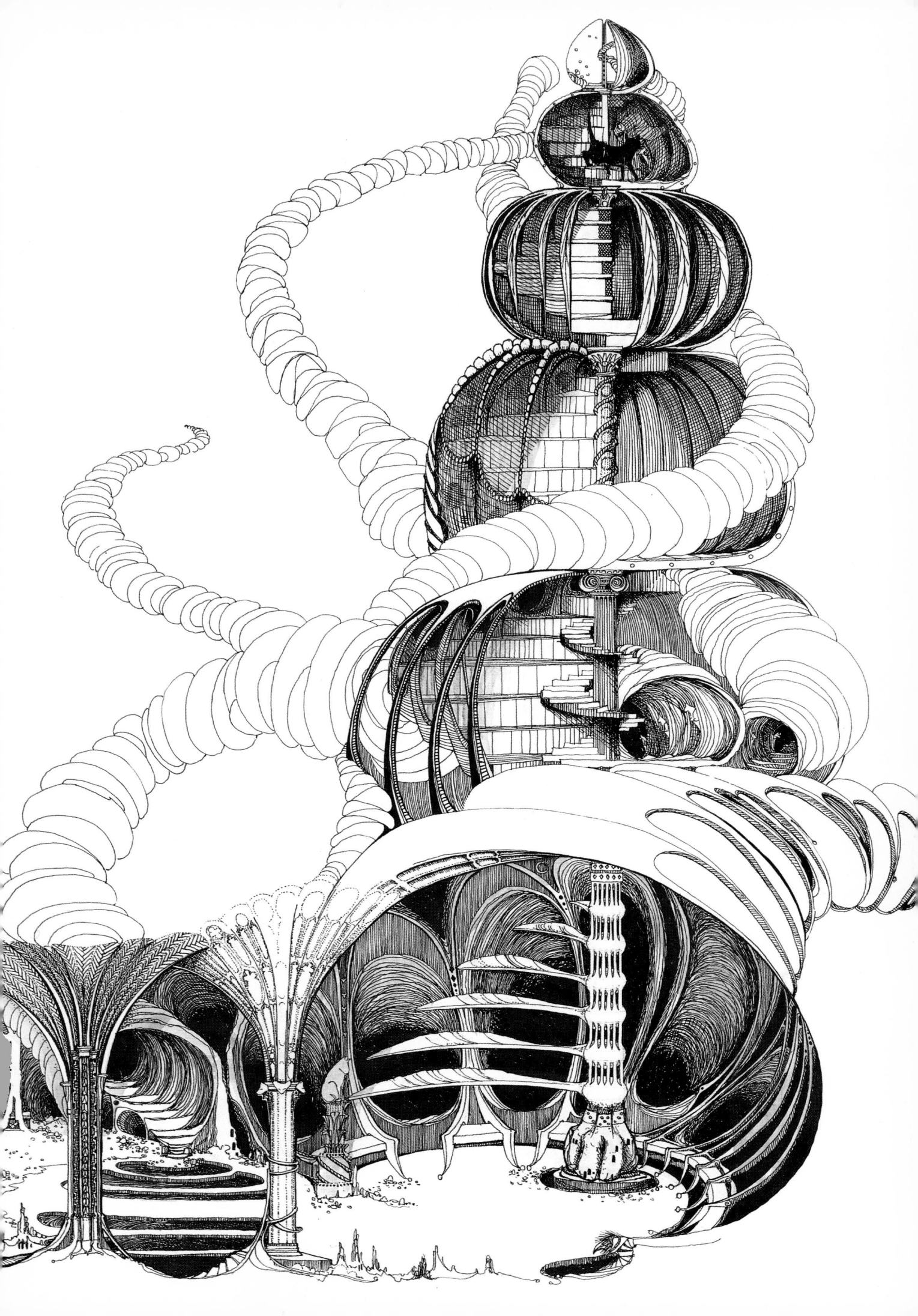

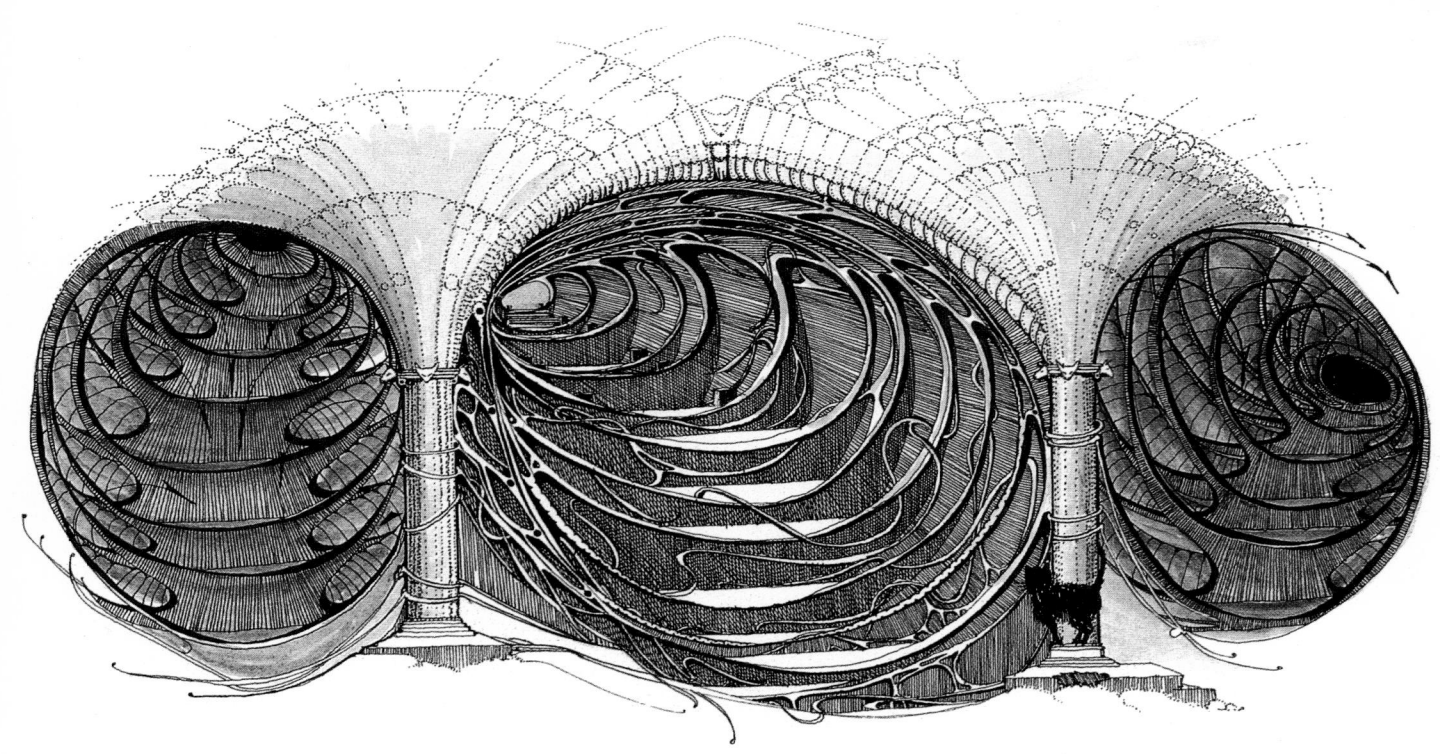

A flight of steps at the end of the tunnel led up towards the light. It was the light of day but not the dappled summerlight of the woods. Nearing the top, Caspar caught sight of a world so different from his own that he could only stare in astonishment.

For as far as he could see, there was no sign of life in this strange country – no sound, no movement. An eerie silence lay across the land like a misty cloud. Gazing up, he saw two enormous mushrooms swaying against the sky, as if floating in the air, and wondered what weird and enchanted kingdom this could possibly be.

Suddenly, the steps beneath his paws cracked open and the walls of the tunnel began to move. Caspar stiffened with fright as, one by one, fleshy mushrooms forced their way through the earth, closing in on him like a creeping army. A shower of stones rattled down behind. Without stopping to think he sprang to the top step and the edge of the unknown world.

. . . all was still and silent.

Frosty air iced his whiskers as he poked the tip of his nose out of the tunnel. It certainly was a most peculiar country. Mosses and ferns smothered the ground. And everywhere there were the sinister mushrooms, growing even as he watched.

Caspar looked across the fields. Far away, he saw a frozen river. Beyond it lay a village and there, too, all was still and silent. Only the mushrooms swayed and danced above the roof tops. High overhead, the crumbling walls of a castle looked as fierce and forbidding as the ancient crags they crowned.

A bridge spanned the river and on it, tiny in the distance, Caspar thought he could see statues. Curious as ever, he set off across the fields towards them. It was a precarious journey, made more difficult by cracks that suddenly split the ground beneath him, as a new army of mushrooms burst out of the earth.

14

Jumping from rocky ledges to mossy banks and down steeply sloping hills, Caspar eventually found himself halfway down a valley where, as if provided for this very quest, a rope bridge snaked its way across a chasm to the bridge of statues. Stepping gingerly on the swaying ropes, Caspar made his way across.

It was a long time before he was able to set paw on firm ground again and, relieved that this part of his journey was now over, he bounded happily on to the stone bridge over the river.

Caspar inspected the statues. Each one was of a cat. Why cats? He was puzzled. Then his ears twitched with excitement as an extraordinary idea came to him. Cats? Cats! Could this strange land be the undiscovered Secret Kingdom of the Cats? The very Camelot that so many brave creatures before him had tried – and failed – to find?

Just imagine if he, Caspar, should be the one to discover it. What a hero he would be!

"I'll go as far as the village," thought Caspar, "and then I'll go home."

When Caspar arrived in the village, the first thing he noticed was the faint but reassuring scent of his own kind. The houses were exactly of the size a cat would make for himself, but when he knocked at the doors nobody answered his calls. It was with a slightly uneasy feeling behind his ears that Caspar realized that the village was deserted: he was completely alone.

Meanwhile, the mushrooms were growing more and more thickly, cutting him off from the bridge and the way back home. They towered over the houses, and squeezed themselves through the roofs and chimney stacks. He would have to move on, but there was no road out of the village; only the frozen river wound its way past the ruined castle and on into the bare, jagged mountains. He made up his mind to follow it.

Carefully, he picked his way upwards, past the empty houses clinging to the banks and ridges above the frozen waterfalls. He shivered as the river led him higher into the icy air. Once, cutting across a gorge, he lost his grip and went skidding and sliding and squealing to the edge of a waterfall. Only the sharpness of his claws saved him from a terrible drop to the icy rocks below.

17

Scrambling back on to the track, he climbed higher up the mountain. The air was so thin here that he could hardly breathe, the ground so cold that all feeling had been frozen from his paws.

Passing through a cave, Caspar found that the track suddenly stopped. Before him lay a staircase, winding up the mountainside for as far as he could see. It suggested that someone had already travelled this way, towards some certain destination. It was a comforting thought and made Caspar feel a little less lonely.

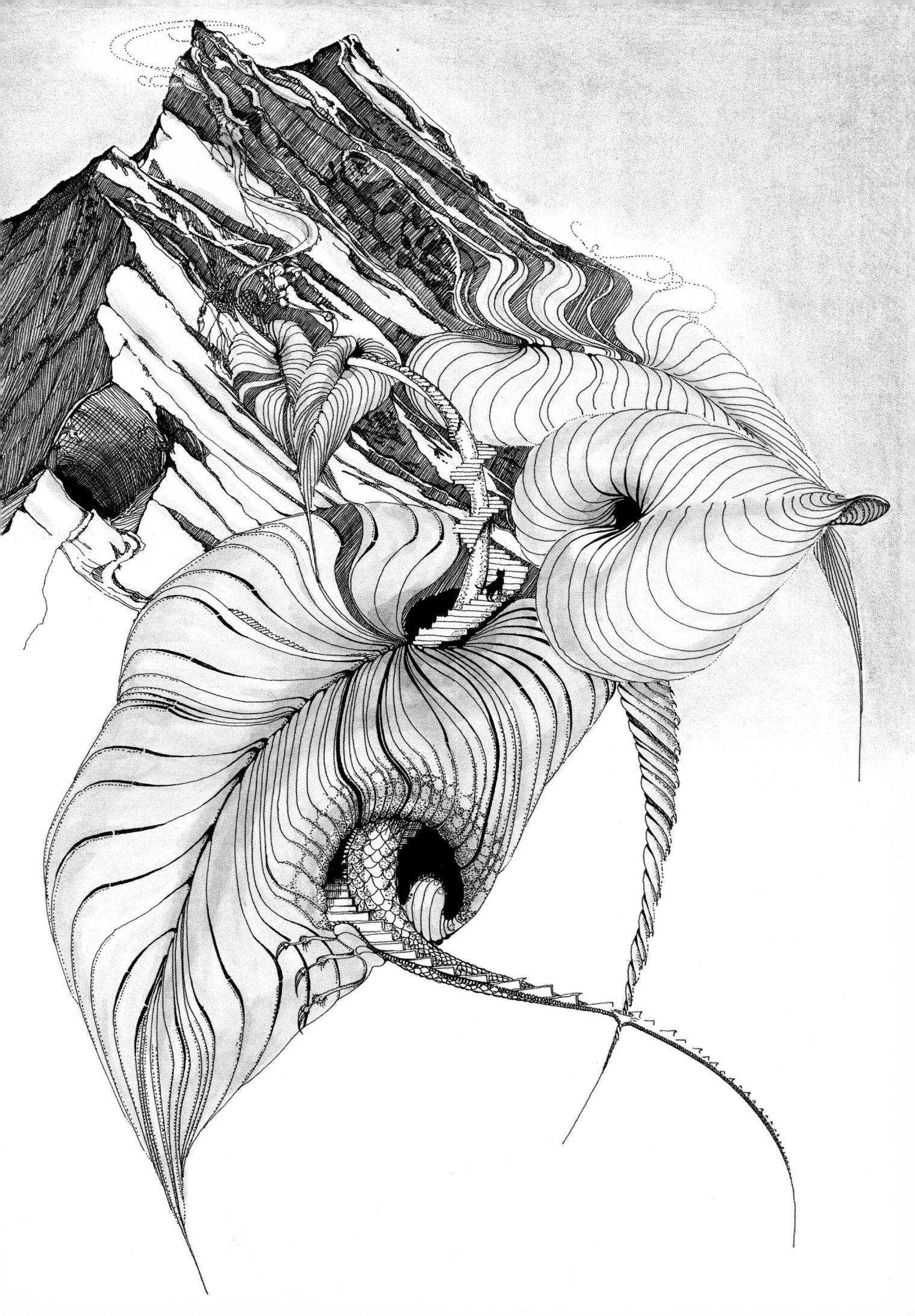

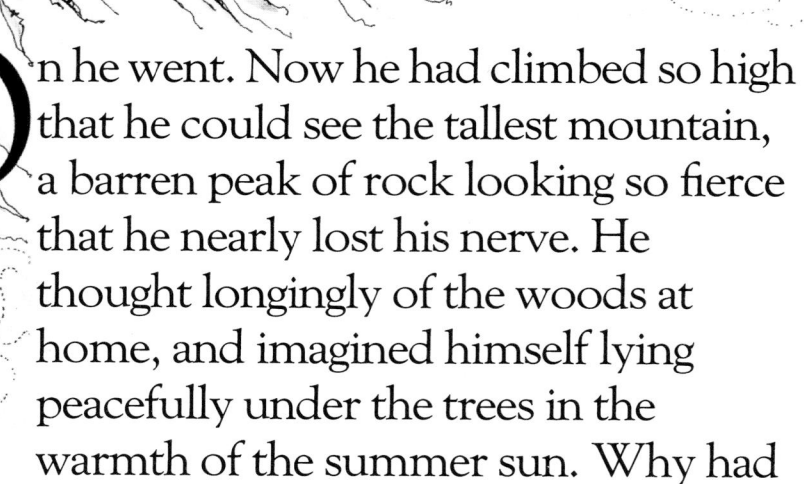

On he went. Now he had climbed so high that he could see the tallest mountain, a barren peak of rock looking so fierce that he nearly lost his nerve. He thought longingly of the woods at home, and imagined himself lying peacefully under the trees in the warmth of the summer sun. Why had he been so reckless, why had he ever begun this adventure?

The steps here were slippery and much more difficult to walk on. At first, Caspar thought the glistening, glass-like surface was ice and placed his paws carefully on each polished step. Then he looked again and realized he was wrong. Stiffening, he sniffed the steps ahead. There was a strange smell about them, a metallic smell mixed with the scent of an animal that Caspar did not recognize. Slowly, a horrifying thought came into his head. The more he thought about it, the more he knew it to be true. These were not steps at all; he had been climbing a stairway of living flesh . . .

Caspar was shaking with fear so much that it was all he could do to save himself from tumbling down the mountainside. But there was worse to come. As he tried

20

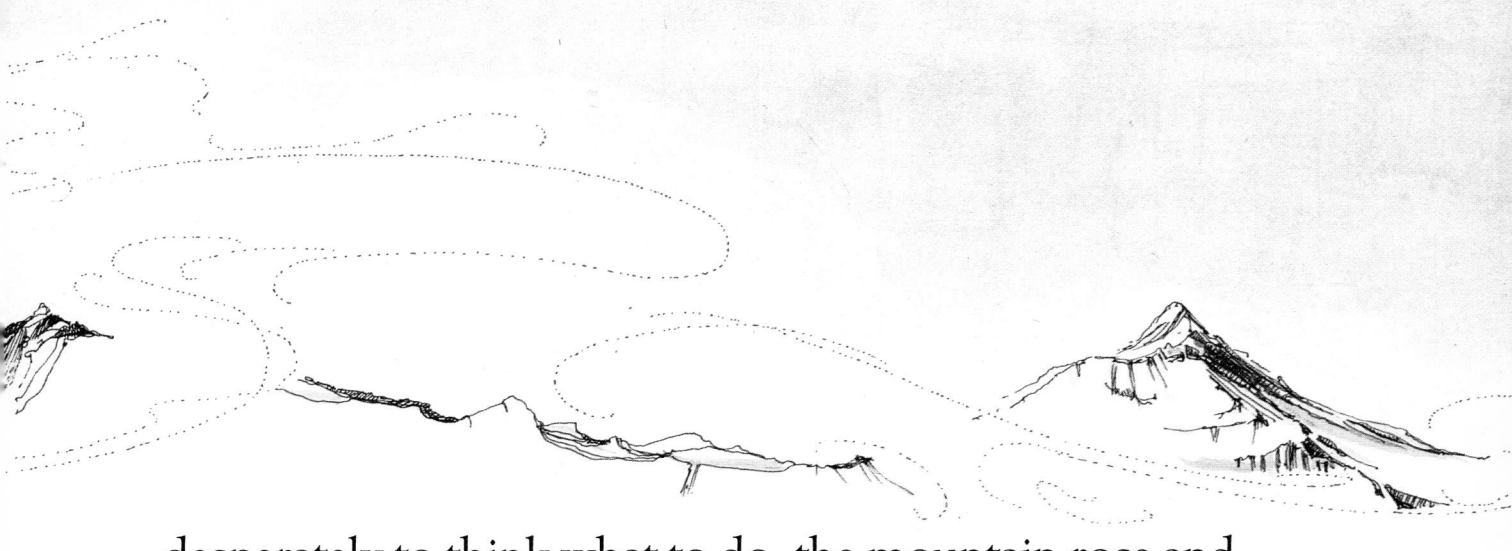

desperately to think what to do, the mountain rose and heaved itself from side to side.

Then there came a loud and terrible roar, the most terrifying sound he had ever heard. It came from the rocks above and echoed round the mountains. Caspar's fur stood up so straight that he looked like a little black bristle-brush. Rigid with fear, he knew he had to jump off the scaly stairway but, before he could move, it rose into the air like a surging wave, sweeping him high above the peaks and into the clouds.

Looking down, he saw, in one dreadful moment, an awful sight. Coiled round and round the mountain peaks was the tail of a monster, so huge that the mountains themselves seemed to be a part of its gigantic body. Caspar had been walking along the back of a dragon!

He had never dreamt such a monster could exist. Its massive tail lashed the craggy peaks and as it did so, he could see ruined castles and palaces embedded in its ugly spines, buildings torn up from the ground in the dragon's wake. A shadow fell across him and, looking up, Caspar saw a giant claw, talons drawn, poised above his head. Beyond the claw was the snarling head of the dragon, breathing fire like an angry volcano.

21

Caspar saw a giant claw, talons drawn, poised above his head. Beyond the claw was the snarling head of the dragon, breathing fire like an angry volcano.

There was no time to think. Caspar shut his eyes and jumped. He landed with a jolt on a narrow ledge of rock. The dragon's head swung slowly to and fro, searching for him, smelling him out through clouds of sulphurous steam.

Caspar looked for somewhere to hide, and saw an outcrop of rocks high up on the cliff-face. He sprang from boulder to boulder up the mountain and crouched behind the rocks, trembling.

Then he saw the dragon's spines rising high above the peak, like the rigid black prows of warships. Before the spines came the head, snorting, searching him out. One dreadful claw scraped the mountainside, hunting its victim, each vicious talon drawing nearer its mark. There was no doubt now that Caspar had been seen, for those awful eyes were looking straight at him. It was only a matter of seconds before the dragon claimed its prize.

When he first heard the rumble and felt the deep vibrating shudder beneath his paws, Caspar imagined it to be the dragon drawing breath, and he braced himself for whatever was to come. What happened was unexpected. From somewhere far below, from the depths of the mountain, came a thunderous rush of hot air that forced itself out of the peak.

Like a planet exploding, the mountain erupted and broke into a million fragments of rock. A scorching jet of flame shot Caspar high into the air and sent the dragon screeching through the sky.

As if in a dream, he found scenes of his past life flashing through his mind in a moment that seemed to have no end. He saw himself back under the tree on a sunny afternoon, chasing mice around the barn, snugly curled up beside a winter fire. Then he was falling, falling, falling . . .

Bravely, he opened one eye. Valleys and hills rose to meet him as he braced himself for a bumpy landing which, when it came, was as soft as falling on a cushion. He had landed in the cap of a giant mushroom and was being rocked like a baby in a cradle. Above, the sky was as blue as a mountain lake. Below, flowers had begun to spread a faint carpet of colour over the hills. At first, Caspar thought he was dreaming. He could hear the sound of gushing water, and his nose twitched as the delicious fragrance of meadow plants came wafting over him – milk vetch, allheal and codlins-and-cream, all mixed together in the warm, sweet scent of summer fields.

Purring with pleasure, Caspar peeped out of the cradle. It was no dream. Something remarkable had happened in the cold and desolate kingdom. The silent, wintery wasteland had become a flowering landscape pulsing with life and warmth. Why? Where was the clue to this transformation? Looking up, he saw the craggy, broken peak of the volcano in the distance and, with a shudder, remembered the dragon. But where *was* the dragon? Caspar searched the sky and hills, but the dragon had vanished as if it had never been.

Now Caspar could hear the distant crack of melting ice. Everywhere, spring was returning. Flowing from the stem of the giant mushroom which had cushioned his fall, he saw a stream of bright clear water, the source of the river, winding its way between brilliant banks of flowers. Fish, bright as the polished stones of the river-bed, glided through the water, darting past fishermen's bait to leap the falls and swim on, out of sight.

Pausing only to amuse himself by trying to catch some bubbles in the wink and spray of the river, Caspar jumped out of the mushroom-cap and set off downstream.

Everywhere, spring was returning.

Some fish were leaping and diving under the spray of the first waterfall, but when they saw Caspar trotting along the bank they flicked their golden tails at him in a friendly way and swam slowly forward. It was as if they wanted him to follow.

Caspar ran along the bank, but since the fish could swim much faster than he could run, he stopped to rest on a large, boat-shaped leaf. From here he surveyed the kingdom. How beautiful it was! Marble palaces rose from the dark cypress groves beyond the water. A staircase of malachite and jasper led down to the river. Far away, he could still see, above ranks of pines, the crags of the mountain he had climbed.

As Caspar sat there daydreaming, the fish played leapfrog, flying high over each other, twisting and arching like dolphins. They were waiting for him. Caspar would have liked to stay longer; it was warm and comfortable in the sun. But just as he was thinking of settling down, the leaf snapped off its stem and landed with a splash in the water. Caspar shook the drops of water off his nose and tail and, to his surprise, found himself afloat on board the leaf, making headway downstream. "A boat trip," he thought. "Whatever next?"

Perched high on the prow, Caspar skimmed along the river, spinning and circling between the tall rushy banks. On either side, giant mushrooms bowed their massive canopies, a silent guard of honour.

As the leaf-boat glided downstream, the river widened into a shadowless lake, where the sight that met his eyes made Caspar blink with astonishment. Everywhere he looked there were cats, cats of every kind and colour – topaz, coral and crimson. They were magnificent creatures, with eyes that shone with the brilliance of stars. These were the kings and queens of the Secret Kingdom, the rulers of dreams from tales his grandfather had told him.

The boat drifted on, and all the while the air trembled and hummed with a familiar sound – the soft thunder of a thousand purrs, filling the air. The cats were lining the banks of the lake as he entered their domain, and waiting to salute him as he passed. They did not speak or move, they simply looked at him. And as he stared up at their wise and shining eyes, he understood that his coming here from the otherworld had saved their land from the dragon's rage, and that they were offering him their thanks.

Caspar longed to stay and talk to the cats, to tell them
of his adventure and to learn about the Secret Kingdom.
He called out again and again but his efforts were in vain.
The cats seemed not to hear, and his cries were lost in the
wind that was relentlessly blowing the leaf-boat further
and further away from them.

Caspar turned to take one last look and to call again,
but the creatures had merged into the landscape, immobile
as the mountains and hills surrounding them.

The wind rushed down through the valley, blowing
the leaf-boat faster and faster across the water to the mouth
of a gorge at the end of the lake. Jagged rocks loomed up
on all sides, the water grew more and more turbulent, and
Caspar's frail craft was tossed in all directions towards a
swirling whirlpool.

Caspar held on tightly and watched with terror as his
boat spun round and round, faster and faster and then
down, down into the vortex of the pool, to the dark
depths below.

37

With a soft thud, the boat came to a sudden stop and
Caspar looked up, startled and a little dazed. The
whirlpool had disappeared; only a small boat-shaped leaf
lying between his paws tickled his nose as he lay snugly
among the roots of an old tree. The evening sun was warm
on his coat as he sat up, yawned and smiled. Then he
arched his back, stretched and turned right round before
curling up into a ball and settling down to sleep.

Where Caspar has come from you can never be sure.
He may have been to the Secret Kingdom, or he may have
been sound asleep. For Caspar is a mysterious cat and
keeps these things to himself.

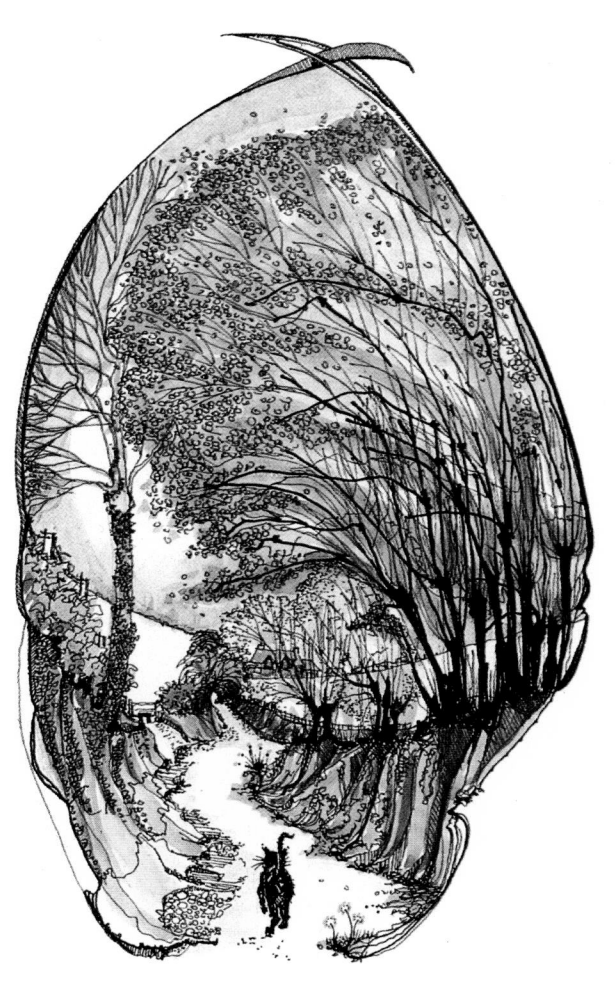

destroying angel (Amanita virosa)

rufus milk cap (Lactarius rufus)

milk vetch (Astragalus glycyphyllos)

mountain cat's-ear
(Gnaphalium dioicum)

dragonroot (Calla palustris)

allheal
(Valeriana officinalis)

milk parsley

(Peucedanum palustre)